£2.75

DESIGNED BY BRUCE MCNALLY
AND LES SKINNER
ILLUSTRATED BY
MANHAR CHAUNAN
PAM STOREY
JO LAWRENCE
SUE VENNING
WRITTEN BY
JOCELYN STEVENSON

A HENSON ORGANISATION PUBLISHING
BOOK PRODUCED IN ASSOCIATION
WITH GRANDREAMS LTD.,
JADWIN HOUSE, 205/211 KENTISH TOWN
ROAD, LONDON N.W.5

PRINTED IN HOLLAND

ISBN 0 86227 150 9

Welcome to the opening of
FRAGGLE ROCK

MEET THE FRAGGLES

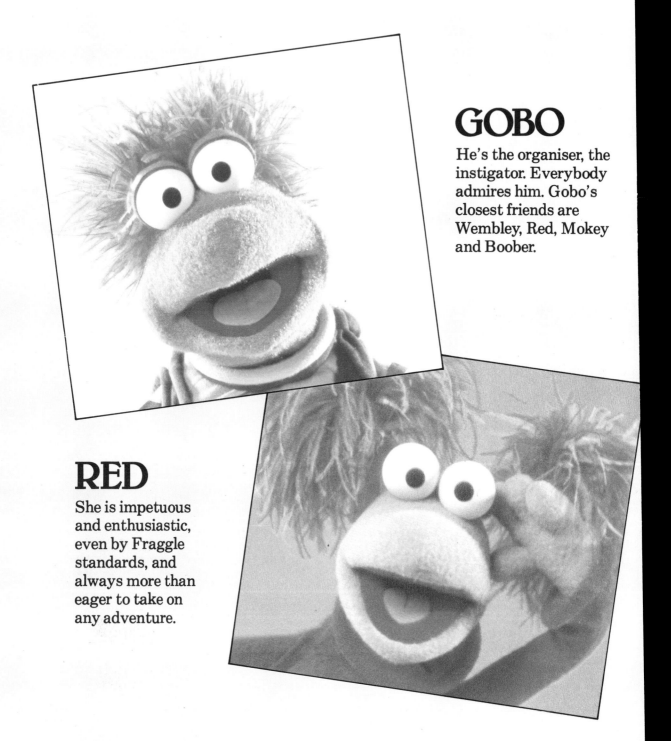

GOBO

He's the organiser, the instigator. Everybody admires him. Gobo's closest friends are Wembley, Red, Mokey and Boober.

RED

She is impetuous and enthusiastic, even by Fraggle standards, and always more than eager to take on any adventure.

WEMBLEY

He's the kid brother of the group. The word Wembley is an ancient Fragglish word meaning "small, insecure and desperate to please".

MOKEY

Now this Fraggle is a dreamer. She is also sensitive, observant, quiet and extremely artistic.

BOOBER

This Fraggle is chronically pessimistic and depressed. As far as Boober is concerned, April showers bring nothing but colds and fever.

Travelling Matt

After leaving Gobo his maps and the only copy of his book "History of the Universe, Part 1", Travelling Matt Fraggle left Fraggle Rock to explore Outer Space. It took him no time at all to make his first discovery — the world "out there" is inhabited primarily by Silly Creatures, multi-sized, two-legged beings with bizarre habits. For instance, by holding up an upside-down bowl on a stick, these creatures can make water pour from the sky. Also, they entertain themselves by watching flat Silly Creatures who live inside a box; they feed round, shiny objects to the Pavement Creatures who are rooted to the ground; and they unquestioningly obey the magic Beast with Three Eyes, one red, one amber and one green. Uncle Matt records his discoveries on postcards which he sends back to his beloved nephew, Gobo. Gobo considers these postcards to be scientific documents. His friends, particularly Red, consider them to be hooey. Nevertheless, Matt feels he is doing Fraggledom a great service, and he will continue to do so until he can find his way back home.

"Dear Nephew Gobo..."

Even as you read this, Gobo's Uncle Travelling Matt is exploring Outer Space, studying the habits and customs of the Silly Creatures (a group of strange beings, of which you are one — unless, of course, you're a Fraggle). Matt relates his impressions of this bizarre world to Gobo on postcards which he sends back from every place he visits. Here are some of Matt's most recent postcards. Do you know what Matt is seeing? Do you know where he's been? Answers on page 60

Dear Nephew Gobo,
The other day I w
walking along, looking f
a bite to eat when I
found it - the most gigant
Doozer construction eve
Why, a Doozer tower
like this could feed all th
Fraggles in Fraggle Rock
for days! At least, that
what I thought until I
tasted it. The food out he
is terrible!
Love, your Uncle
Travelling Matt.

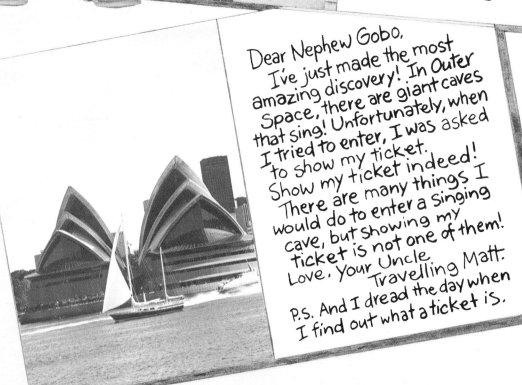

Dear Nephew Gobo,
I've just made the most
amazing discovery! In Outer
Space, there are giant caves
that sing! Unfortunately, when
I tried to enter, I was asked
to show my ticket.
Show my ticket indeed!
There are many things I
would do to enter a singing
cave, but showing my
ticket is not one of them!
Love, Your Uncle
Travelling Matt.

P.S. And I dread the day when
I find out what a ticket is.

Dear Nephew Gobo.
Today I had the fright of my life! I was on a boat on one of the Fraggle ponds out here in Outer Space when I saw it! – The hugest Gorg imaginable! And it was just about to thump me!
Fortunately, I was too quick for it, and I escaped.
Love,
Your Uncle
Travelling Matt.

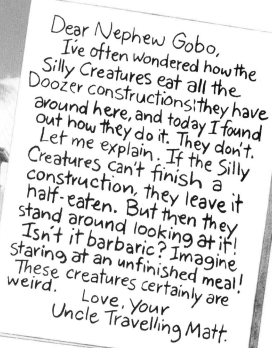

Dear Nephew Gobo,
I've often wondered how the Silly Creatures eat all the Doozer constructions they have around here, and today I found out how they do it. They don't. Let me explain. If the Silly Creatures can't finish a construction, they leave it half-eaten. But then they stand around looking at it! Isn't it barbaric? Imagine staring at an unfinished meal! These creatures certainly are weird.
Love, Your
Uncle Travelling Matt.

Dear Nephew Gobo,
I love a nice furry pet, but I wouldn't want it to live on my head! Would you? I actually discovered some creatures who keep their pets on their heads! I asked one of them if it was comfortable to keep his pet on his head. Do you know, he didn't even answer? His pet was asleep, and he didn't want to wake it up. Strange... Love, Your
Uncle Travelling Matt.

Gobo

So, being brave and daring and adventurous comes naturally to Gobo and are qualities his friends all admire and respect.

They also respect the fact that every few days Gobo goes into the room at the End of the Tunnel to collect the postcards from his uncle.

Gobo Fraggle is the leader of the group. He wasn't elected or anything; he just sort of got the job. Red tries to take it away from him now and then, so sometimes they share it, but most of the time, Gobo's the one who decides what everyone is going to do.

Gobo is an explorer. He comes from a long line of explorers — his very own Uncle Travelling Matt even left Fraggle Rock to explore the far reaches of Outer Space, the Ultimate Quest.

This job would be easy if the room were uninhabited, but it's not. A great furry, four-legged beast with sharp teeth lives there and makes it his business to chase Gobo. So maybe Gobo has earned the position of leader after all.

ROCK MAZE

See how quickly you can find your way through the maze to the Gorgs' Garden. Route on page 60.

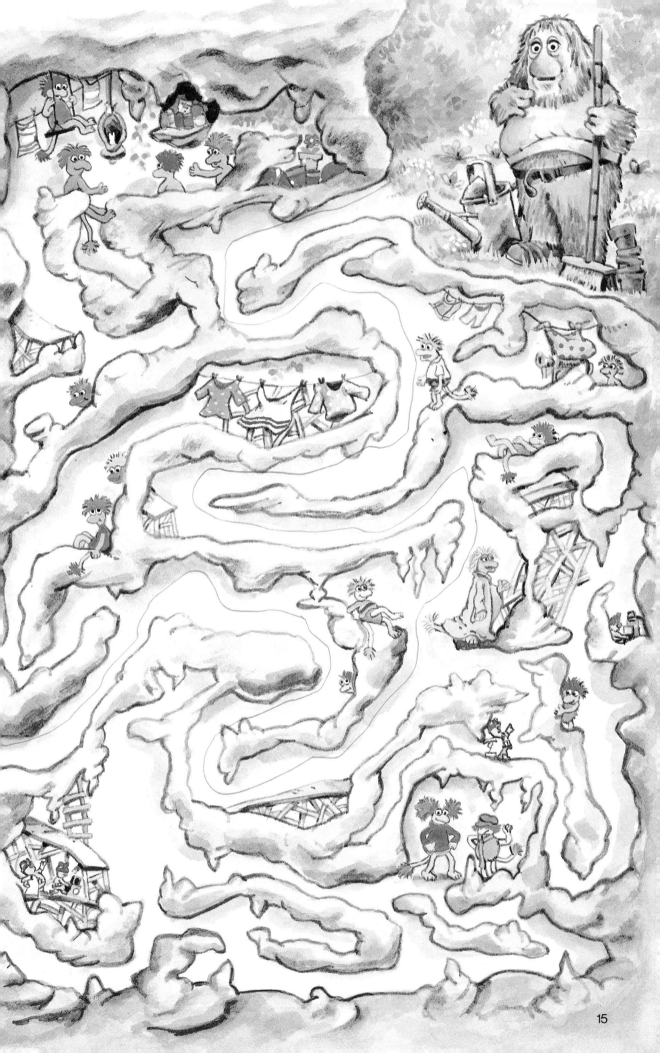

Wembley

Wembley Fraggle has never been good at deciding. In fact, "to wemble" is a useful Fragglish word meaning "to go back and forth from one thing to another without deciding on anything." In these pictures, Wembley is wembling about whether to stand or lie down or look right or left or straight ahead. In the morning, he wembles about which shirt to wear though he has only two and they're both exactly alike.

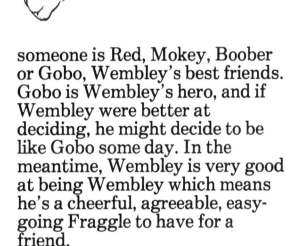

someone is Red, Mokey, Boober or Gobo, Wembley's best friends. Gobo is Wembley's hero, and if Wembley were better at deciding, he might decide to be like Gobo some day. In the meantime, Wembley is very good at being Wembley which means he's a cheerful, agreeable, easy-going Fraggle to have for a friend.

Part of the reason Wembley has such a hard time making decisions is that he is genuinely eager to please. So he doesn't like to disagree or decide something which might make someone unhappy — especially if that

An Adventure a Day Keeps Tomorrow Away

"You know, Wembley," said Gobo Fraggle to his friend and constant companion, "I could use a radish right now."

"Yeah, me too," agreed Wembley — partly because he was hungry and partly because he always agreed with Gobo.

So the two of them ran to the pantry to find a nice, juicy radish. Instead they found Red and Boober.

"But there are no radishes," said Red Fraggle.

"Not a single one," moaned Boober, counting again to be sure.

"What's wrong with Mokey?" asked Gobo.

Picking radishes was Mokey Fraggle's job, and her four Fraggle friends found her lying on her bed with a mosspack on her head.

"I don't feel quite up to picking radishes today," said Mokey, which meant she felt worse than she'd felt in a long time. Mokey was not one to complain or shirk work.

Her friends tiptoed out of the cave. "What should we do?" asked Boober, his stomach growling with hunger.

"We've got to help Mokey," said Gobo. "One of us will go up to the Gorgs' Garden to pick some giant radishes to tide us over until she's back on her feet."

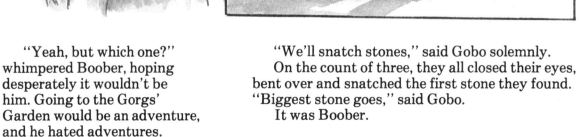

"Yeah, but which one?" whimpered Boober, hoping desperately it wouldn't be him. Going to the Gorgs' Garden would be an adventure, and he hated adventures.

"We'll snatch stones," said Gobo solemnly.
On the count of three, they all closed their eyes, bent over and snatched the first stone they found.
"Biggest stone goes," said Gobo.
It was Boober.

Meanwhile, up in the Gorgs' Garden, Junior Gorg was carefully carving a face in a giant pumpkin shell.

"Well, Mr. Pumpkin, now that you've got a face, maybe you will talk to me," he said. "I need someone to talk to around here. It gets lonely being a prince," Junior sighed.

Just then, Boober sneaked out of Fraggle Rock and headed towards the radishes. He was shaking like a jelly on a plate.

"Why do I have to be the only prince in the universe, Mr. Pumpkin?" bellowed Junior just above Boober's head.

Boober jumped four Doozers into the air and ducked into the nearest hiding place, which just happened to be the pumpkin shell.

"Oh help," cried Boober as he curled himself up and tried to hide under his hat.

Junior leaned in closer to the pumpkin. He didn't know a Fraggle was hiding inside.

"What did you say, Mr. Pumpkin?"
"Get me out of here!" moaned Boober.
"But you just got here," said Junior.

Back in Fraggle Rock, Boober's friends decided that he'd been gone long enough. "It's been six Doozer towers since Boober left," said Red.

"We'd better investigate," said Gobo.

"Right," agreed Wembley.

"Knowing Boober, he's probably cowering somewhere unable to move," snorted Red.

"Oh, please don't destroy me," begged Boober, cowering in the pumpkin shell, unable to move.

"Why would I want to destroy you, Mr. Pumpkin?" asked Junior. "I was the one who made you in the first place."

"This is an adventure," wailed Boober. "I want to go home."

"But this is your home," insisted Junior. "You're my friend and you can live here forever and ever."

Meanwhile, Red, Gobo and Wembley peeped out into the Gorgs' Garden. "I'm going to die!" yelled Boober's voice.

"That's Boober!" whispered Red.

"Over there!" and they set off towards Junior.

"But why would you want to die, Mr. P? I can call you Mr. P, can't I?" Junior good-naturedly patted the pumpkin, bouncing the terrified Boober around inside the pumpkin. "You're going to be my best friend ever."

"Oh, please don't hit me," moaned Boober.

Boober's best friends hid. "Be prepared for anything," warned Gobo. Red nodded. So did Wembley, but he added a gulp because he was scared.

Junior smiled at the pumpkin shell. "I didn't hit you," he said. "I just gave you a nice, friendly pat like…"

Gobo and his friends ran out of hiding and scurried around Junior's feet.

"Fraggles!" shouted Junior and dropped the pumpkin shell.

"Let's go!" Red and Gobo grabbed Boober and everyone ran towards Fraggle Rock.

That night, they sat around the fire in Gobo and Wembley's room and told Mokey the whole story.

"Well, Boober, you had some adventure," she said, smiling.

"And I'll never have another one," said Boober, "if I can help it."

THE END

Red

Red Fraggle is the kind of Fraggle someone watches and then says, "Now there's a really energetic Fraggle who knows where she's going and what she wants to do." And then, CRASH, Red runs right into a stalagmite.

does well (which, in her opinion, is just about everything) she likes swimming the best. Red's other bests in her life are Mokey, her best friend; Gobo, her best sparring partner; pigtails, her best hairstyle, and the Triple Sideways Over Under Back Twist, her best dive without holding her nose.

But that doesn't stop Red. It's certainly not her fault the stalagmite didn't know enough to move.

Moving is one thing Red never stops doing except maybe when she's asleep — but even then she keeps moving in her dreams. If she's not diving or running or sliding down the slide, she's balancing a racket or having an adventure or doing her job which is cleaning the pool. Of all the things that Red does and

VISIT THE TRASH HEAP

To play this game you need a dice, and each player must have a counter or marker. You throw a 6 to start. If you land on a path stone with a RED number, you must take the dirt track to the opposite end and rejoin the path, even if it means going to a lower number. Starting on number 1 you follow the path round. The first player to reach the Trash Heap is the winner.

Mokey

This is Mokey Fraggle writing in her diary. She might be writing a poem such as,

"Sing hi, sing lo
for the bright red glow
of a radish that's far
from a Gorg's big toe."

Or she might be writing a song, or perhaps something more profound and observant such as, "Red's hair is like a sunset in the Gorgs' Garden without the sun and without the Garden," or "I must remember to tell Boober that feeling down has nothing to do with how short you are."

Mokey is a dreamy, graceful, thoughtful, artistic and endlessly helpful Fraggle. If you're in trouble or need advice (but don't think it's bad enough to see the Trash Heap), talk to Mokey. She'll always help you — it may not be the kind of help you want, but it just might be the kind of help you need.

When she's not helping someone, Mokey likes to sing or paint or write or take long walks.

Her job is gathering giant vegetables (from the Gorgs' Garden) for the Fraggles to eat. She loves the Gorgs' Garden, but isn't at all fond of the Gorgs. "If it weren't for them, the Garden would be perfect," she often says. If it weren't for them, there wouldn't be any Garden, but Mokey hasn't thought of that and probably never will.

"Dear Nephew Gobo..."

Gobo's Uncle Travelling Matt is still exploring Outer Space, studying the habits and customs of the Silly Creatures (a group of strange beings, of which you are one). Matt relates his impressions of this bizarre world to Gobo on postcards which he sends back from every place he visits. Here are some more of Matt's most recent postcards. Do you know what Matt is seeing? Do you know where he's been? Answers on page 60

Dear Nephew Gobo,
Though I'm no expert on Doozer constructions, I know what I like.
Unfortunately, none of the constructions in this world taste good, but some of them are quite nice to look at.
I particularly liked this tower. And so do the Silly Creatures - they come from miles around to admire it.
Love, Your
Uncle Travelling Matt.

Dear Nephew Gobo,
For the first time in a long time, I feel at home in this strange world. At last I found something normal, something without a hint of bizarreness. It was a rock! A rock that changed colour - just like the caves at home! What a discovery! Nephew, I can't tell you how refreshing it is to find something ordinary out here!
Love, Your Uncle
Travelling Matt.

Dear Nephew Gobo,
I was wandering through a very hot and dry place, when I came upon the most amazing stalagmites I've seen in a long time. They were growing right out of the sand! How they managed to grow in such a climate, I'll never know. Oh well, I guess there are a few things I'll never know.
Love, your
Uncle Travelling Matt.

Dear Nephew Gobo,
I wish you'd been with me today to see the amusing Fraggle pond the Silly Creatures have to play in. It's got its own built-in slide - a slide of impressive dimensions, I might add. According to a strange creature called Information, the best way to slide down this slide is in a barrel! Sounds like fun!
Love, your
Uncle Travelling Matt.

Dear Nephew Gobo,
Today I came upon a Gorg's castle, and it had the most enormous radishes I've ever seen. How did those radishes get so big? I asked myself. The answer hit me - no Fraggle had ever been able to gather the radishes. Why? Because these Gorgs grew them on top of their castle instead of in a garden. I'll let you know if I figure out a way to gather one of them. Love Your
Uncle Travelling Matt.

Boober

If Fraggles had middle names, Boober's would be "Uh-oh." Boober Fraggle is almost always worried about something or if not worried, then frightened or depressed. Boober's tendency to see the down-side of life provided him with a fairly good education, though.

Boober realised many days ago that he should know as much as possible about everything in order to know all the things there were to worry about. So Boober knows a lot of things that most Fraggles don't know (or care) about, such as

"A knot in the tail can bring good luck" and "Never look over your left shoulder or between your legs at a rolling boulder" and "Stale puddle water can cure the most stubborn bruises."

Another thing Boober knows a lot about is laundry. Doing the laundry is Boober's job, and he chose it because, in his words, "It's so wonderfully tedious and boring." Boober sometimes feels that if it weren't for him, no one would truly appreciate how good they felt.

GUESS WHO THIS IS?

Join the dots and colour in
this picture of a little fellow who works
down at Fraggle Rock

Sprocket

This is Sprocket. People think he's a nice, friendly dog. Fraggles think he's a horrible, terrifying beast who lives in Outer Space, in the Room at the End of the Tunnel. It is from this room that Gobo Fraggle must collect the postcards from his Uncle Travelling Matt. Every time Gobo goes through the Hole into Sprocket's room, the brave Fraggle must face the terrible beast. If Sprocket sees Gobo, he barks and chases him out of the room. Sprocket thinks chasing Gobo is fun. Gobo doesn't agree.

Doozers

The Doozers are about six inches tall, or knee-high to a Fraggle. They live and work — mostly work — inside Fraggle Rock. They build and build and build magnificent bridges, towers, monuments, roads and anything else they can dream of. They use vegetable protein sticks, processed by mining turnips and radishes in the Gorgs' Garden as their building material. If you stopped long enough to realise it, you might say, "You know, those Doozers do the things they do because of the dreams they dream." Even though the Fraggles don't pay much attention to the Doozers, they do have a keen interest in their architecture — it tastes delicious! Fortunately, the Doozers don't mind that the Fraggles eat their constructions.

In fact they appreciate it because it gives them the space in which to build better ones.

Doozer Construction Game

This Doozer has left behind his lunch box in the bottom far corner. Can you help him find the shortest route to his lunch? Also, how many Doozers do you think are working on this construction? Answers on page 60.

START

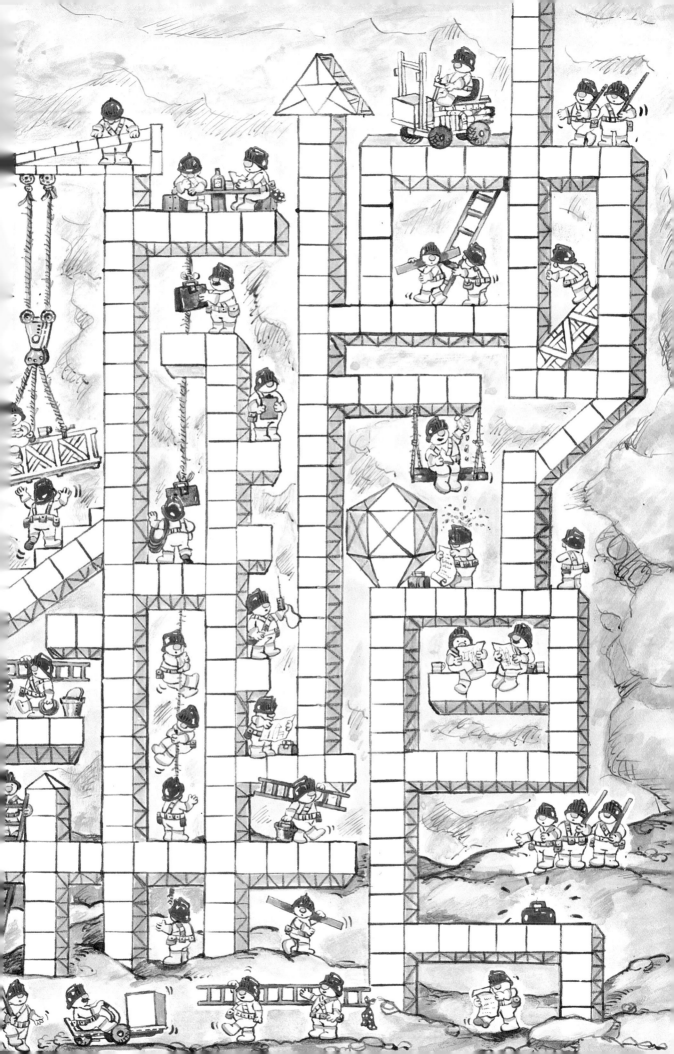

The Gorgs

Gorgs, at 22 feet tall, are fifteen times the size of a Fraggle, and they live in the crumbling remains of a castle just outside Fraggle Rock. There are three remaining members of the species — Pa, Ma and Junior. Pa and Ma are King and Queen of the Universe because they said they were and because there's no one around to disagree.

Junior's not interested in the Universe. He's only interested in Fraggles. Whenever Junior's not doing all the work his parents would do if they weren't so busy ruling the Universe, he tries to catch Fraggles.

Consequently, the Universe
doesn't care about Gorgs at all,
but the Fraggles do.
It's very hard to gather giant
vegetables while being chased by
a moving mountain. Almost as
hard as it is to be a moving
mountain chasing very fast
Fraggles.

Pa, Ma and
Junior Gorg

TEST YOUR SKILL

There are 15 differences between the two pictures below. Using your skill, write down as many as you can; or else cheat and look them up in the back of the book on page 60. Then use your talent to colour in the bottom picture.

The Trash Heap

Trash Heap lives in a pit in the woods behind the Gorgs' castle. She is a living compost heap — an ancient collection of old grapefruit rinds, grass clippings, tin cans, coffee grounds, potato peel and assorted trash which one day mysteriously came to life. The Fraggles brave the dangers of the Gorgs' Garden to seek the Trash Heap's advice in times of trouble. The Trash Heap is an oracle. She sees all, she knows all, she is all. The Trash Heap may be the Creative Force behind the universe. Then again she may not be.

She is definitely home for Philo and Gunge, her two rodent companions. They act as her interpreters, her agents, her best friends. Philo and Gunge are the only ones who are allowed to call the Trash Heap by her first name, Marjory. If you go to see the Trash Heap, Philo and Gunge will let you know when your time is up: "The Trash Heap has spoken!"

The Big, Horrible, Smelly, Ugly, Terrible Gooey Mess

Gobo, Mokey, Wembley, Boober and Red were in the Great Hall playing by the Fraggle Pool (though to be perfectly accurate, Gobo, Mokey, Wembley and Red were playing and Boober was worrying about them) when they first heard the noise. Groongagroongagroonga.

It sounded like something very big far away or something very small close up — it was hard to tell because the echoes in the tunnels of Fraggle Rock did confusing things to sounds.

Boober, who was always on the lookout for strange and therefore worrisome events, immediately concluded that whatever it was, it would destroy Fraggle Rock and life as they knew it. Gobo, Mokey, Wembley

and Red — who, like most Fraggles, put playing, singing, laughing, swimming, diving, frolicking, romping, leaping, eating, sleeping and almost everything else ahead of worrying — figured it was a distant Doozer platoon working on a massive construction and the groongagroonga noise was probably one of their bigger machines. Red smacked her lips just thinking about it. "Imagine a Doozer construction so big that we might not be able to eat all of it at once."

"Yeah!" agreed Wembley, smacking his lips too.

"After we finish this game of Pile the Pebble, let's play Splish and then see if we can find the delicious construction," suggested Gobo, finishing off his pile.

GROONGAGROONGA!

"By then we'll be hungry enough to eat anything!" Mokey put the prettiest pebble she could find on the top of her pile. Then she gently pushed the whole thing into the pool — 'Splish!' Mokey was delighted. The last two times she'd made a pebble pile, she'd done something wrong and it went 'Karplonk'. But this time it was perfect. She watched her friends nervously prepare to push in the piles. 'Splush!' went Red's — close but not quite. 'Splish!' went Gobo's (as usual) and 'Plinkplinkplink' went Wembley's.

"Oh, I'll never get it right," sighed Wembley.

"Sure you will," comforted Mokey. "It just takes..."

"Listen!" interrupted Boober who'd been straining his ears over the splishes and plinkplinks to hear whatever it was that was on its way to destroy them all. "It's getting closer!" Groongagroongagroongagroonga! No one wanted to admit it but the sound wasn't like any other Doozer machine they'd ever heard. Instead it was a frightening huge sort of noise.

"It sounds like a Gorg!" Boober couldn't think of anything worse.

"But no Gorg could ever get in Fraggle Rock," reasoned Mokey. "Gorgs are way too big!"

"But Boober's right," said Red, which was surprising because she almost never agreed with Boober. "This noise sounds big like a Gorg."

As they spoke the GROONGA—

GROONGAGROONGAGROONGA GROONGAGROONGA got louder and louder and then...it stopped.

The five Fraggles, who by now were huddling behind a boulder, peeked out to have a look. There, in the middle of their Great Hall, sat the biggest, ugliest and most mysterious Gooey Mess imaginable. So massive it entirely covered the swimming hole, the Mess had tufts of hair sprouting from the most peculiar places and at the very top of its mountainous bulk sat its face — if that's what you wanted to call it. It was actually three squinting red eyes and a gigantic ferocious mouth. And out of the mouth came a continuous cloud of green foul-smelling vapour.

Boober suddenly realised he would rather faint from fear in the safety of a distant cave than there in the Great Hall. "Listen, Gobo," he reasoned dizzily, "you have enough on your hands without an unconscious Fraggle. I'm getting out of here."

Unfortunately, the Mess noticed Boober running for cover and with a tremendous grunt, it lunged for the desperate Fraggle with one, fat, globby paw. Fortunately, it missed. Grabbing a pawful of boulders instead, the Mess stuffed them into his mouth, chewed noisily and swallowed.

Boober no longer cared where he fainted.

"Boober. Boober wake up!" cried Mokey desperately patting his nose.

Gobo, Mokey, and Wembley watched the ravenous mass turn its hungry gaze in their direction.

"Y-y-y-you leave us al-l-l-l-one!" cried Gobo, so frightened he stuttered.

Groongagroongagroonga — the Mess shifted its weight and moved slowly towards them.

"I can't get Boober to wake up!" screamed Mokey.

"Boober!" said Red, grabbing his tail. "Wake up now!" And she gave a mighty yank. Boober woke up all right, and without stopping to say, "Where am I?" he ran out of the Great Hall, dragging Red behind him.

"Run!!!" yelled Gobo, and he, Wembley and Mokey followed their terrified friends.

"What is it?" whispered Mokey, holding her nose.

"Well, it's not a Gorg," said Gobo.

"It's horrendous!" said Red, her pigtails shaking from the shock of it all.

"What are we going to do?" asked Wembley.

"Die! We're all going to die!" moaned Boober.

Except for the Mess and the five Fraggles, the Great Hall — usually filled to overflowing with busy Fraggles and Doozers — was deserted. The Doozers had quietly, calmly and quickly evacuated the cave for more out of the way tunnels, and any Fraggles who'd happened to see or smell this massive Mess enter the Hall, had long since run for their lives. Only Gobo, Mokey, Wembley, Boober and Red were brave enough — or dumb enough — to stay. Make that Gobo, Mokey, Wembley and Red.

The five Fraggles flew into Gobo and Wembley's room and collapsed on the floor, panting.

"What is that thing?" asked Red.

"I don't know, but we've got to get it out of here," said Gobo.

"Where did it come from?" asked Mokey. "What does it want with us?"

"Listen!" whimpered Boober.

They heard the terrible sound of their Great Hall being chewed up.

"I'm going to have a look," said Gobo. He sneaked down the tunnel and peered into the Great Hall — or what was left of it.

The Gooey Mess sat in the middle of the cave grabbing Doozer constructions, boulders, stalactites, stalagmites — whatever it could get its horrible flabby paws on — and stuffing them into its cavernous mouth.

Whenever it caught sight of a frightened Fraggle, it roared, burped and lunged. Seeing Gobo, it reached out and almost grabbed his leg, but he ducked into a crevice just in time.

"I'm going to see the Trash Heap," said Gobo when he returned to report what had happened. "We need all the help we can get. That thing isn't going to stop until it eats us all!"

"Well, I'm going with you," said Red.

"Me, too," said Mokey, Wembley and Boober together. They didn't want to be left behind, just in case the Mess decided to eat their room with them in it. For the first time in their lives, crossing the Gorgs' Garden to get to the Trash Heap didn't seem frightening at all — not compared to crossing a Great Hall filled with a Gooey Mess.

The five Fraggles huddled at the entrance to the Great Hall, terrified.

The Mess seemed to be sleeping. As it snored, the foul green cloud wafted gently back and forth across its head, like waves on a beach. Now and then it grunted and shifted positions, but all three eyes were tightly closed.

"I wish that thing hadn't come here," whispered Mokey.

"If wishes were radishes," quaked Boober, "we'd all be stuffed."

Gobo, Mokey, Wembley, Boober and Red held hands and tiptoed into the Hall, keeping as far away from the Mess as possible. They were halfway to Gorg Tunnel, when one of its little red eyes opened and saw a five course dinner walking across the cave. Groongagroongagroonga! It reached out, trying to grab Red by the tail. She ducked behind one of the few remaining boulders, pulling her friends with her.

The Mess's paw oozed around the rock, picked it up and deposited it in its mouth. While it was smacking its lips, the Fraggles ran for their lives and were almost all the way to the Gorgs' Garden before they stopped to catch their breaths.

"That was not fun," panted Red.

"You said it," agreed Wembley.

"But I wish you hadn't," moaned Boober.

The five frazzled Fraggles crept out into the Gorgs' Garden. Junior was in the radish patch, hoeing.

"The Gorg almost looks nice after that thing back there," shuddered Red.

"Yeah, but not that nice," said Boober, running as fast as his legs could carry him. He'd noticed that the Gorg had noticed that they were noticing him.

"Fraggles!" cried the Gorg. But thanks to Boober's natural reaction to something 15 times his size, the Fraggles were well out of reach.

"Someday, I'll get you Fraggles!" declared Junior, and he went back to planting radishes.

"What is it I can do for you little Fraggles?" crooned the Trash Heap, rising to her full height.

"Yeah, spit it out," chimed Philo and Gunge, the Trash Heap's two ratty companions.

The Fraggles stared awed at the Heap's all-knowing leaves, her wise coffee grounds and orange peel. If anyone could help them, she could. Gobo was the first to speak.

"Oh, Madame Heap, something awful has happened. A thing..."

"...a big horrendous blob..." interrupted Red.

"...that smells terrible," added Boober.

"...has invaded Fraggle Rock," continued Gobo. "It's eaten the Great Hall."

"...and it's trying to eat us!" cried Mokey. "Can you help, please, oh please?" And moved by the excitement of the moment, she grabbed Wembley and hugged him to her.

"Oh please?" echoed Wembley.

"A big Gooey Mess?" questioned the Trash Heap. "Looks horrendous? Smells terrible?"

"What's wrong with that?" asked Philo.

"Sounds charming to me," added Gunge.

"Quiet, boys," scolded the Trash Heap, her eyes flashing. "Can't you see this is serious? Can't you see these Fraggles are frightened out of their little furry heads?"

Philo and Gunge could see, so they fell silent.

"Now, let me think," continued the Heap. "I'm done thinking," she said after a moment. "My advice to you is don't be frightened. Don't run away."

"What!?!" cried all five Fraggles. They thought perhaps she hadn't heard what they said.

"But how can we help it?" asked Red, trying not to sound disrespectful. "If we don't run away, this horrible Mess will EAT us. EAT!" And Red demonstrated her point by chewing nervously on her tail.

"I heard you. I heard you," said the Heap. "But you must trust me. I'm acquainted with Gooey Messes. I happen to know they feed on fear."

"Hey, Marjory, how do you know that?" asked Philo.

"How many times do I have to tell you," answered the Trash Heap, "I know everything?" She gently bonked Philo on the head with an old tin can, only she missed and hit Gunge instead.

"Now listen," she said, turning back to the Fraggles. "Don't be afraid of this Mess and it will go away. Guaranteed."

"The Trash Heap has spoken!" yelled Philo and Gunge, who was still rubbing his head.

The Trash Heap sighed and sank into the earth.

"You heard her," said Gobo. "We can't be afraid."

"Right," said Wembley.

"But fear is all I have to offer," moaned Boober.

"Me, too!" said Wembley.

"No, no," said Mokey soothingly. "We've got to do what the Trash Heap says."

"Let's practice on the Gorg," said Red.

"Let's not and say we did," whimpered Boober.

But despite Boober's rather appealing suggestion, the five Fraggles joined hands and bravely faced the Gorg.

When Junior saw five Fraggles just standing in his garden, he got so excited he jumped up, tripped on his hoe and crashed to the ground.

"It worked!" cried Gobo. "Come on, gang, let's go!"

As they neared the Great Hall and smelled the overwhelming odour of the hungry Gooey Mess, their confidence almost left them completely. They could hear it slowly moving around the gutted Hall, looking for food. Groongagroongagroonga.

"Okay, everybody," said Gobo. "Stash your fear where the Mess can't see it...or smell it — though I don't see how anyone could smell anything while it's around."

It wasn't easy, but they all managed to get rid of their fear. Mokey and Wembley swallowed theirs; Gobo put his at the back of his mind; Red pretended she'd never had any in the first place; and Boober — well. Boober closed his eyes and imagined that he was bigger and messier than the big Mess itself. It worked, but only if he kept his eyes closed.

So the five of them joined hands and walked confidently into the Great Hall. Boober, his eyes tightly closed, tripped on Wembley's tail a few times, but otherwise, their entrance was fairly fearless.

When the Mess heard them coming, it turned and stared with all three eyes. The Fraggles just stood there.

"Go away!" said Gobo bravely.

"We're not scared of you!" said Red surprised that she actually meant it.

The Mess moved towards them, but they held on to each other and refused to budge or look the least bit flustered.

"Get out of here!" demanded Mokey, genuinely angry because of all the damage the thing had done.

"Who do you think you are?" asked Wembley.

"You great, big, smelly, horrible, ugly, terrible, awful Gooey Mess!" added Boober, desperately imagining that he was even greater, bigger. smellier, more horrible and uglier at least equally terrible and awful.

The Mess looked at them. They stood their ground. It shook its blobby head, not knowing what to do. For some reason, brave Fraggles always made it lose its appetite. So, with one last burp, it rolled out of the Great Hall and disappeared down a long tunnel.

"We did it!" cried Gobo.

Boober opened his eyes and fainted. Now that the Mess was gone, he could safely be afraid again. But so could everyone else, if they wanted to be. But they didn't have time. They had to fix up the Great Hall so they could play and swim and dance and sing and think twice before ever being afraid of another Gooey Mess, no matter how great, big, smelly, horrible, ugly, terrible and awful it was.

THE END

FRAGGLE SUPERSTITIONS TO LIVE BY

Boober's mottos, "It's worth being scared" and "It's better to be safe than non-living". Boober knows more ways to be safe than any other Fraggle because he reads his Book of Superstitions whenever he can. Here are a few words of wisdom from this sacred (to Boober) Book:

A cross-eyed worm looks at you,
Wear your lunch and eat your shoe.

Knot your tail for luck.
(The more knots, the more luck).

When you see spiders on a Rock wall, count them:

One's a letter
Two's a wish
Three's a fortune
Four's a fish.

Flower pots are lucky. So are walking sticks, yo-yos, blankets and orange socks.

It's good luck to hear a Hufty-tufty before it hears you.

If you hold your elbow and tickle your foot, you will never meet a three-headed Flerk with rust-coloured spots.

If you find a flat pebble, throw it in the air and you will have all the pebbles you want for the rest of the day.

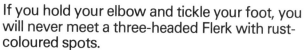

ANSWERS

Travelling Matt 1

Eiffel Tower, Paris, France.
Sydney Opera House,
Australia.
Statue of Liberty, New York,
U.S.A.
Parthenon, Athens, Greece.
Guardsman, London, England.

Travelling Matt 2

The Leaning Tower of Pisa,
Italy.
Ayers Rock, Australia.
The pyramids, Egypt.
Niagara Falls, Canada and
U.S.A.
Taj Mahal, India.

Test Your Skill

1. Red's thumb missing.
2. Red's fourth toe missing.
3. Red's bow missing.
4. Mokey's right hand missing
from Red's shoulder.
5. Mokey's eyes moved.
6. Mokey's pendant missing.
7. Mokey's foot missing.
8. Boober's lost one end of his
scarf.
9. Gobo's wearing his hat with
a feather.
10. Gobo's lost his jacket
pocket.
11. Gobo's lost one part of his
scarf.
12. Gobo's lost his tail.
13. Wembley's lost his tongue.
14. Wembley's thumb missing.
15. Wembley's lost a button off
his jacket.

The Rock Maze

Doozer Construction Game.

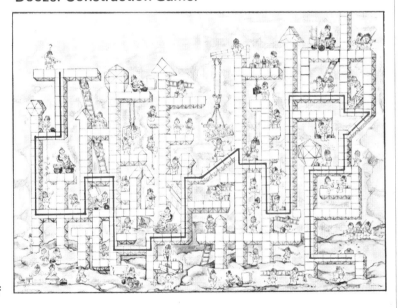

See you all very soon down at Fraggle Rock